CW00802726

For Jeff, Ruaridh and Immy - my world - HK
Thanks to Sarah, Katy, Hazel, Pips, and everybody who still believes
in pixies and magic... - CW

2024 written by Hazel Knox and illustrated by Chris White
Hazel Knox & Chris White are part of HB Publishing House.
The Night Pixie
HB Publishing House, 21, NG13 7AW
British Library Catalogue in Publication Data: a catalogue record for this book is
available from the British Library.
ISBN: 9781068642777

The Night Pixie

Hazel Knox

Dandelion Farts

The night air is so cold that the tips of my wings have frozen. I've been hovering above the same frosty flower for too long, dithering over whether to take it home. Dandelions make yummy tea, but they also make Granny fart like a badger. Before the cold turns me into an ice pixie, I use my flint axe to chop down the yellow flower and cram it into my gathering bag. I've survived Granny's wind problem before; I can do it again.

My eyes strain, trying to pick Mum out from the garden's murky shadows. Our oak tree is the biggest dark shape. The moss-covered treehouse peeks out from its branches. Granny says when she was young, human children used to play in it, but that was a long time ago. Mum's in the vegetable patch. Her night shimmer makes the air around her ripple.

She's probably looking for radishes.

I hate radishes.

While she's distracted, I fly higher to spy

1

on the gardens around us. Next door, two fox cubs take turns rolling down a grassy bank. I glide further up, above the fence, to see the woods in the distance. How many night pixies are there right now, having adventures?

If I go just a little higher, I'll be able to -

"Star!" Mum hisses across the grass. "Stay low!"

I drop down below the fence line, and Mum darts over. "What were you doing?!"

"Sorry," I say. "I was just looking."

"We've talked about this. The human at the end of our garden doesn't have her lights on at night, but other houses do. What if you were seen?!"

"Sorry," I say again.

"The sun will be up soon. We'd better get inside," Mum says.

"Couldn't we stay? For a little bit?"

"We're night pixies," she says, "which means we come out at...?"

"Night," I sigh.

"And we never go out during the...?"

"Day."

"Because...?" she prompts.

"Day is danger."

"That's right, because day is full of HUMANS!" she cries. "They want to trap us, keep us in cages. And when the sun's up, there's no darkness for us to hide in, no night shimmer to make us harder to see." Her voice changes. "I love you, Star. I don't want what happened to your dad to happen to you."

"I know," I say quietly.

She takes my hand and we fly to the base of the oak tree. "Ready?" she asks. I nod, and she pushes on a worn spot. A piece of bark springs inwards, leaving just enough room for us to squeeze through.

"At last!" Granny screeches. "I'm starving! Wasting away. One day, you'll take so long, you'll come home to a pile of bones."

"We've only been an hour," Mum sighs.

Granny is magically refreshed by the sight of the dandelion. She totters over, her hazel walking twig tapping on the floor. Granny's so old her wings don't work anymore.

"Mmm," she says, sniffing the flower in my bag. "Any chance of some tea before bed? Helps me let go of the night's stress."

That's not all it makes her let go of.

"I'll light the twigs," Mum says, "again."

Granny winks at me and makes herself comfortable in her chair. Mum spent a week carving it out of a fallen branch.

I look through my other gatherings from tonight and pick out a sad-looking holly berry left over from winter. Kneeling by the fire, I squeeze the berry's last drop of juice onto a flat piece of bark, then scratch the colour around with a twig. It gradually turns into a picture of our tree, surrounded by other trees.

"Very nice," Mum says, looking over my shoulder. She hands me an acorn cup of tea and a slice of radish. "Have this, then time for bed."

When she turns away, I stuff the radish into my bag. I'll slip it back outside tomorrow night. The sweet tea's gone in seconds. Before long, I'm lying in my dock leaf hammock, listening to Mum snoring gently and Granny 'letting go' from the other side of the room.

"Paaarp! PAAAAARP! Pfft."

It's just been the three of us for as long as I can remember. Dad went missing when I was a baby. Mum told me he liked to go out gathering just before dawn. He thought the herbs tasted best then, especially parsley, his favourite. Only one early morning he didn't come back. Just disappeared. All Mum found was his bag next to a human footprint. That's why she's so nervous about being outside, especially if there's any hint of daylight.

"Parp. Pfft." Although inside has its problems too.

It hasn't always been like this. When Mum and Dad were young, this oak tree was on the edge of the woods. The trees were full of night pixies. As long as it was dark, they'd be outside. All those families have gone now as more human houses were built, but we can't move because Granny can't fly anymore. It's not her fault, but I wish things were different. Only leaving the tree to gather, no-one to play with - life isn't exactly exciting.

I sigh and turn over. My tummy rumbles. I'm wondering whether I should have forced the radish down when a delicious smell hits me. My nostrils flare, and I take a huge sniff, sucking as much air up my nose as possible.

Mm mmm.

I sit up.

Sniff. Sniff. SNIFF!

Mm, mmm, mmmm!

The dandelion farts are long gone. This smells like freshly-dug earth mixed with squirrel-stored nuts and just-fallen plums. And something else, something new. I wish my nostrils were bigger so I could cram more in. My tummy growls in agreement.

I have to find out what it is.

2

The Smell Hunt

My mouth waters. Whatever is making the incredible smell needs to be in my belly, right now.

I peek over at Mum's hammock. Each time she breathes out, a long strand of hair dances above her face; she's definitely asleep. Pushing the moss cover aside, I swing my legs out of the hammock and let my wings unfold. A crack of sunlight invades as I pull on my crocus dress.

The smell leads my nose straight to the hatch in the ceiling. On the other side, running up the centre of our oak tree, is an escape tunnel - in case an animal gets in. Like the time a mole charged in behind me after gathering. It ate our entire stock of dried apple and chewed Granny's pea pod slippers. Mum had to entice it out with a worm. Granny never wore the slippers again.

I ease the hatch open. It squeaks, and Granny stirs. Only my wings are moving as the whites of her eyes stare through the dark. I desperately try and think of a good reason why I'm up, but the only thought in my head is 'find the smell'. I brace myself, but Granny closes her eyes again. There's a quiet 'pfft' and then snoring. She must have been dreaming. Thank the moonlight for that.

Scrambling onto the tunnel's daisy chain ladder, I pull the hatch closed behind me. It's damp and dingy. A splinter of light blinks high above, where another hatch opens into bushy branches at the top of the tree. There's no room to spread my wings, but I don't care because the passageway is filled with the delicious scent. This must be the right way. I climb up and up and up the ladder. My nose never stops sniffing, and eventually, I reach the point where the smell is strongest. But there's nothing here!

When I press my face up against the wall of the tunnel, I see a chink of light. The smell makes me brave, or stupid maybe, but either way, I pull at a loose bit of bark. My ears wiggle, a sure sign of danger nearby, but I'm too focused on my grumbling tummy to care. I scratch and pull at the wall until there's just enough space for me to squeeze through.

The light is blinding. I blink and rub my eyes until they re-adjust. It's day, but I'm not outside. It takes a few seconds to figure out I'm in the human treehouse that sits in the oak tree branches!

It's huge, four times the size of our home at the bottom of the tree. Sitting on the floor on a dotty plate is a wedge of food unlike anything I've ever seen. There's a layer of brown spongy stuff, then brown creamy stuff, topped with another spongy layer and lashings of the creamy brown on top. The smell wafting from it makes me all floaty.

There's a loud gasp. I look up and the floaty feeling evaporates. I'm staring straight at a wide-eyed human with a blue dress and a wet face.

A HUMAN!

And she's looking right back at me!

It's a pixie trap. How could I have been so stupid? I broke the unbreakable rule and went out in daylight.

Day is danger!

I keep still, except for my ears wiggling their warning. The human is less than five pixie lengths away. She's sitting cross-legged on the floor, looming over me. I'm not even half the size of her head.

I've only ever seen a human from far away: the grey-haired one that lives in the house at the end of the garden. This one is smaller with brown curly hair.

She takes a white square out of her pocket and uses it to dab her eyes and wipe her face dry. Then, the pixie-trapping, curly, sniffy human shuffles closer.

Why didn't I listen to Mum?

Rose

A frightened squeak escapes from my mouth.

"I won't hurt you," the human says, springing back.

That's exactly what a pixie-trapper would say, but I'm distracted by another waft of the delicious brown food. My wings vibrate, and I can't help glancing at it.

"You can have some if you want," she says.

I'm not that stupid. It must be poisoned.

"I'll eat some first," she says, "so you know it's okay."

Clever.

I snatch another look and a hungry groan sneaks out.

"My dad made it," she tells me. "It's guilt cake."

It looks almost as good as it smells, but my dad got taken by a human, like her. So no thank you, I won't have any. I take a step backwards, towards the hole leading into the tree.

Very slowly, the girl reaches towards the plate, takes some guilt cake and puts it in her mouth. I take another step back, but the sweet scent makes my legs wobble.

She finishes eating.

I stay where I am. I really should go.

She pushes the plate over with her fingertips, keeping as far away from me as possible. The smell wafts my way. It's so good that I can't help licking my lips.

Would a little bit be so bad? I'm close to the escape tunnel, and I'm pretty sure if she makes a grab for me, I can get away.

I shake myself. This is a human! The biggest danger to pixies. Snatcher of fathers. Of course I shouldn't take any, no matter how delicious it smells, how sweet, how mouth-wateringly tasty...

I can't resist. I have to have the guilt cake. Lunging forward, I grab a handful and shove it straight into my mouth. Shooting stars! My taste buds are dancing.

I didn't know it was possible for something to taste this good. It makes the time I had a whole raspberry to myself seem dull. I grab two more handfuls and cram them into my mouth. The spongy bit is amazing, but the creamy bit is out of this world.

"Good?" asks the girl.

"So good!" I say, crumbs spraying everywhere. Oops, I just spoke to a human.

"The icing on the top is my favourite bit," she says.

I don't reply. Instead, I eat and eat. The girl never moves, and gradually, I forget about her and enjoy the guilt cake until I can't squeeze any more in. I slump down on the floor, feeling like an overripe apple that's fallen off the tree. I'm too full to move. Helpless. This must be how she's going to trap me.

But she doesn't. Instead, she asks, "What's your name?"

"Star," I say. I must stop talking to humans. "What's yours?" Oops!

"Rose," she says.

"That's pretty," I say. Rose really isn't what I thought humans would be like.

"So's Star," she says and nods at the cake. "Do you want any more?"

"No room," I say, my hand resting on my belly. "I love guilt cake!" Rose laughs. "It's chocolate cake. Dad made it because he felt guilty."

"Chocolate," I repeat. "I like chocolate cake. Why did he feel guilty?"

Rose sighs. "He and Mum left me here with Aunt Mo so they could go away for the weekend. That's why I was upset. I've only met her once, years ago. I'm not good at talking to new people. I came up here so I didn't have to."

I lick my fingers one at a time while she speaks. "You're talking to me," I say.

Rose wraps her arms around her legs. "True. You're a little different, though. Star, erm, what are you?"

"I'm a night pixie." I don't think Rose is trying to trap me. Mum said humans are our biggest threat, but this one seems more nervous of me. And nice. And there's no sign of a cage. Even my ears have stopped warning me. Could Mum have got it wrong? Maybe something else happened to Dad.

"Are there more of you?" Rose asks.

"Just me, Mum and Granny in this tree, but most woods have got night pixies," I reply.

Rose's eyes are open so wide they might fall out of her head.

My turn for questions. "Is Aunt Mo the lady with grey hair?"

"Yes. She keeps giving me food and asking me to paint with her. She's an artist."

That sounds like a dream come true. I wonder if Aunt Mo uses berries for paint. "Don't you want to?"

"Not really," she admits.

I can't imagine not wanting to paint. "What do you want to do?"

Rose thinks for a moment. "I like making videos," she says, "but I forgot my charger and my phone's dead."

"I'm so sorry," I say. Poor Phone. Rose doesn't look too upset, though, so I ask, "What's videos?"

She tilts her head to one side. "Moving pictures."

I imagine my woodland painting dancing around. I must look confused because Rose tries to explain. "I have different backgrounds and a light, and I record myself on my phone."

I stare at her, and she keeps talking.

"I can speak when it's just me and the camera, but me and a stranger - not so much."

Backgrounds? Camera? Dead Phone? Moving pictures? I don't have a clue what she's talking about, but I don't want to look silly, so I change the subject. "My mum lets me paint with berries, but she doesn't let me do much else and she NEVER lets me leave the tree in the day."

Being here with Rose, in daylight, is the most exciting thing that's ever happened to me, by moons.

"I'm glad you're here now," Rose says, smiling. "Would you...do you want to come and see Aunt Mo's house?"

4
Day

I fly to the treehouse window. Rose watches me, open-mouthed. Aunt Mo's house is at the end of the garden I know so well. It looks completely different in the daytime: blue sky, green grass, yellow, pink, red, purple and orange flowers, all with their petals proudly open. It's an explosion of colour.

Should I go outside, in the sunshine, while the plants are awake and the birds are singing? Explore a human house with Rose? Have an adventure like I've wanted forever? My wings vibrate at the thought.

But day is danger.

Every night Mum warns me about what lurks outside our tree in daylight hours. The tips of my ears wiggle at the thought. Mum loves me. She wouldn't lie. And what about what happened to Dad?

19

Although Rose doesn't seem one bit dangerous. And no-one knows for sure what happened to Dad. Mum must have got it wrong. My ears settle down. "Yes," I say to Rose before I change my mind, "I want to come."

She claps her hands and scoops up the cake plate. "Yay! Follow me, but don't let Aunt Mo see you."

I'm all for that plan. Inviting one human into my life is enough. Rose holds the door open while I take a deep breath and stroke my wiggling ears, before fluttering outside.

"Stay close to me," she says, but I've already flown down to a patch of sunny grass.

I lie on my back and let the warmth wash over me. It feels like a hundred comforting hugs all at once. At night, the garden feels small and shadowy, but in the daytime it's big and bright. I flutter over to the herb pots by Aunt Mo's door: mint, rosemary and Dad's favourite, parsley.

Instead of hurriedly stuffing shoots into my gathering bag, I hover and look at them, feel the soft fuzz on their open leaves, then smell them.

Day doesn't feel dangerous. It feels amazing.

A creature lands on the mint. It's about the size of my head and looks like a moth. Except smaller, with a delicate pattern of red, black, blue and yellow on its wings. It's the most beautiful thing I've ever seen.

"Star," whisper-shouts Rose from Aunt Mo's door, "stay hidden, remember?"

I nod but I'm too excited to hide. The creature flaps away and I chase it, following its zig zag path to a wooden platform, but it leaves when a bird lands beside us. The new arrival comes up to my chest. Its tummy looks like sunshine and the blue on its head matches the sky. It chirps happily as it pecks. I copy, putting my hands on my hips and bending down to move the seed around with my nose. The bird tips its head to the side and looks at me before it steps over and pecks my foot.

"Ow!"

Peck.

"Ow!"

I dive off the platform into multi-coloured flowers below. The sweet smell tickles my nose, and the happy chaos of buzzing, chirping and singing makes my head spin. Night noise is so different. Darkness brings hoots, snuffles and snaps.

The buzzing gets louder. Black and yellow striped, furry, flying creatures, only slightly smaller than my head, dart this way and that. Granny told me about these ones: bees. They love flowers. They're surrounding me, nuzzling my petal dress!

"Shoo!" I cry. "I'm not a flower!"

The bees scatter. Wow! I must sound really scary.

"Kxxsss!"

Or perhaps it was the big ginger cat that scared them. He's crouched low to the ground, ready to pounce. My ears wiggle, my heart beats faster and I shoot upwards out of the cat's reach. I recognise him. He must be a night and day creature.

"Kxxsss," he spits again, pawing at the air under me.

"Kxxsss."

I guess that confirms my protective shimmer doesn't work in the day. This cat can definitely see me.

"Star!" Rose calls, louder this time, and waves me over to the house. "This way."

I fly over to join her.

"Murphy, shoo!" she hisses at the cat and he stalks off.

I give him a little wave goodbye from behind Rose's shoulder.

"Aunt Mo told me she doesn't like cats in her garden, especially that one," Rose says, opening the door. She peeks in and whispers, "All clear."

I glance back at the oak tree, shake out my wings, and follow her inside. I'm in a huge room looking straight at a picture on the wall. It's dark blue with a brown and green swirl in the middle and three yellow dots. I wonder if Rose could make it move.

"Aunt Mo painted it," Rose says. "It's quite, erm, splodgy."

I'm surprised I notice anything about the room, because my nostrils are flaring again. Sitting on the cloth-covered table is the rest of the guilty chocolate cake. I think I could squeeze some more in now. My mouth waters.

Rose moves towards me as I soar upwards. "Star! No!"

I hover above the cake. There's a perfect slice missing, so I can see all the delicious layers. The icing glistens in the light. It's calling to me.

"Don't!" Rose's voice says from far away.

I can taste it in my mouth, feel its sweetness on my lips. I must have it.

"No!" Rose calls as I launch myself straight at the cake.

SPLAT!

I land with my mouth wide open. Hello, old friend.

"Oh! Hi, Aunt Mo!" I can just hear Rose say through the icing clogging my wiggling ears.

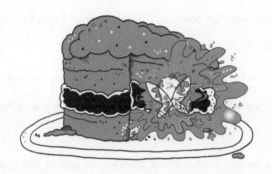

5

The Sucky Sink

I slide down the side of the cake, keeping my mouth open to catch extra icing. Then hurry to the edge of the table and flutter off. Except, I'm so weighed down by chocolate that I splat straight onto the floor.

"Did you shout?" Aunt Mo asks. Footsteps thump across the floor, then stop abruptly. "What on earth has happened to the cake?!"

I scramble under the table and shimmy up one of the legs until I'm hidden under the red and white cloth hanging down. The chocolate all over my hands makes it difficult to hold on, but I wrap my legs around the wood and concentrate on breathing quietly.

"It was...I erm..." Rose stutters, "slipped and fell into it."

"You slipped and fell into it?" Aunt Mo repeats.

"Yes," Rose says. "I'm really, really sorry."

"But you managed not to get chocolate on your clothes?" Aunt

Mo asks.

That is exactly what my mum would have asked. Grown-ups are such lie-detectors.

"Just on my arm. I washed it off. I was about to clean up here when you came in."

Quick thinking, Rose, but I really need you to wrap this up. I'm slipping!

"Well, accidents happen," Aunt Mo says, not sounding convinced.

There's a loud ringing from somewhere else in the house, more footsteps, and then Aunt Mo's voice in the distance.

"Star?" Rose whispers. "It's safe to come out."

Thank the moonlight for that. I release my grip and slide stiffly down the table leg, landing in a crumpled sticky heap on the floor.

"You took the blame," I say, looking up at her. I've never had someone to do that for me before. Rose is nothing like how Mum described humans. She isn't scary, or out to get me; she's lovely.

"Well, you're new to human houses," Rose says. "Maybe you didn't know not to jump in the food."

"I know now." (I knew before, but the chocolate cake made me forget.)

I sit up. Rose wipes the mess off the table and floor. "Can you fly?"

I shake my head, sending a blob of chocolate icing onto the floor she's just cleaned.

"Wait there," Rose says and disappears.

She comes back a minute later, clutching some purple material.

"Jump on," she says. "I'll take you to get cleaned up."

I hesitate.

"It's okay," Rose says. "It's my dress. I'll be careful, but I can't risk Aunt Mo seeing you. I'm not sure what she'd do."

I step onto the dress and sit down. Rose gently wraps me up. The fabric smells like her. A dark, bumpy minute later, she unwraps me and I step out onto the floor of a different, smaller room. There's a little window almost covered by the plants sitting on the sill underneath it, their leaves trailing down. Another splodgy painting hangs on the wall. This one looks like umbrellas in a snowstorm. Everything else in the room is white and shiny.

"You can get cleaned up in here," Rose says.

I stare at her, confused.

"The shower might be a bit powerful, so we'll put warm water in the sink. You can use the hand towel," she says, picking up a huge, pink, fluffy thing from silver pipes on the wall.

I have no idea what she's talking about. What's a sink? It's not raining, so how am I supposed to shower? And there's no fire to dry myself next to.

"Rose!" Aunt Mo shouts from somewhere in the house.

"Wait here," Rose tells me. "I'll be back in a minute." She hangs the pink fluff over one of the shiny, white things and hurries out, leaving me alone and sticky in the new room.

After the whole diving-in-the-cake incident, I need to show Rose I can be a good guest. I want her to like me and this could be the perfect chance. I'm sure I can figure out what to do. That will definitely impress her.

Three large, shiny, white objects loom over me. There's a huge one that stretches across one side of the room. Brightly coloured bottles sit on its edge. 'Shampoo' I can just make out on one. Why would they put poo in a bottle? That's gross!

The tallest white thing is under the window and has the pink towel hanging on it. Next to it is a lower one that looks like a giant version of Granny's chair. I decide to check out the chair. Mainly because my wings are still too sticky to fly, and that one has a handy climbing strip hanging next to it.

I get a grip and pull myself up. Except I don't move. Instead, the soft strip comes shooting down to meet me. And not just a bit, more and more of it piles on top of me, so I have to crawl out, leaving chocolatey stains all over it. I'm not giving up. No way.

I take a running jump and just manage to catch the edge of the white chair.

From there, it's easy to pull myself up. I'm standing on a round platform with a big hole in the middle, and at the bottom of the hole is a pool of water. This must be the sink! Ripe raspberries! What a lucky guess!

My dress is covered in chocolate, so I leave it on and jump straight in. I gasp. It's freezing! I thought Rose said it would be warm! The water quickly turns brown and gloopy as some of the chocolate washes off. How am I supposed to get clean in this?

I look around and spot a metal lever above me. Hopefully that does something. Warms the water, maybe. Thankfully, my wings are now clean enough that I can fly again. I flutter up and land on the silver lever. It moves, but nothing happens. So I jump on it. It moves down and suddenly, lots happens. There's a rumbling whoosh, and more water floods into the sink. The brown gloopiness disappears. This must be right. Except as quickly as it started, the flooding stops.

I try again, but this time, I'm ready. I jump on the lever, and as soon as the fresh water starts pouring in, I dive straight in.

"Argh!" It's still not warm.

Dying dandelions! It's sucking me down!

Oops

I splutter and kick and grab at the shiny sides of the sink. I try desperately to keep my head up, but the spiralling, churning water drags me down. My chest hurts and I can feel the panic rising, when suddenly, everything stops. The water is still. I kick upwards and burst through the surface, taking several big gulps of air, before flying out of the useless sink and collapsing on the floor.

I lie there, staring at the ceiling, until I feel normal again. This really can't be right. Getting clean shouldn't be so...horrible. There must be more to it.

Hang on...the pink fluff! Rose told me to use the towel. How could I have been so stupid?!

The towel must go in the sink. That would stop the sucking down, so I can get a proper wash when the fresh water comes in. I'm going to give it one last go. When Rose comes back, she won't believe I figured it out on my own.

The pink towel is hanging on the tallest shiny, white thing.

I grab the end and pull and pull, flapping with everything I have until it moves. I shoot backwards and FLOP!

It lands on the side of the sink.

One huge push and it falls in.

The towel sucks up all the water but

I guess that's what it's supposed to do.

I give it a soggy stamp to make sure it's secure. I'm red, sweaty and even more sticky, but so close now.

I jump on the silver lever for the last time, with an extra high leap. I can't help feeling smug that I worked this out without any help. Rose is definitely going to be impressed. I happily hop down onto the towel as the water floods in again. It's much comfier. There's no sucking and the towel makes the water level rise so I get a better wash. It's still cold though.

And there does seem to be lots of it. Lots and lots and lots. Sticky willow! It's pouring onto the floor!

I fly out and hover above the unfolding disaster. The puddle is spreading towards the door, and the rumbling and flooding isn't stopping as quickly as it did last time. The silver lever is still down. It must have been the extra high jump!

This is not good. This is definitely bad.

The door opens. "Star!" Rose cries. "What have you done?"

She wiggles the lever, then wiggles it harder. Her face goes red and she starts grabbing all the fluffy towels and throwing them on the wet floor.

I decide it's time to go back to my night life where things make sense, but before I get a chance to fly to freedom, Aunt Mo appears at the door.

"Rose! What on earth?" she shouts.

Without thinking I dive towards Rose and hover behind her as Aunt Mo comes into the room, splashing across the floor to the sink. She grabs the lever, wrenches it up, and the flooding stops. Rose has carefully turned around so her front is towards Aunt Mo, keeping me hidden.

"Why is this in the toilet?!" Aunt Mo cries, putting her hand in the sink and pulling out the pink towel. I peek over Rose's shoulder. The expression on Aunt Mo's face reminds me of how Granny looked when Mum asked her for a foot rub.

Rose coughs. "I erm, slipped," she says. "I'm really sorry,"

"You slipped?" Aunt Mo says, her eyebrows disappearing into her grey hair. "Again?"

"Sorry," Rose says. "Again."

"But why is all this toilet paper on the floor?" Aunt Mo asks. "Did you slip on that too?" She looks closely at the mound of chocolate-stained, soggy climbing strip. "Is that...what is that?"

"It's chocolate!" Rose says. "Nothing else! I cleaned up in here after I fell into the cake."

I peek over Rose's shoulder. Aunt Mo has her hands on her hips. She marches out, leaving us alone.

"Quick!" Rose cries. "Hide!"

I look around desperately, but there's nowhere to go.

Aunt Mo's footsteps are coming back.

I panic.

Proper Painting

I shoot up the back of Rose's cardigan and wriggle upwards until my head pokes out amongst her curly hair. From here I can keep an eye on what's going on. Aunt Mo doesn't seem to notice Rose squirming, because she immediately hands her a long stick with a squidgy bit on the end, and tells her to start mopping.

"I just don't understand how you slipped, dropped a towel in the toilet and then flushed it," she says. "Are you sure you're okay? Is there anything you need to tell me?"

"No, nothing. I'm just super clumsy today," Rose says, mopping vigorously. "I really am sorry."

Aunt Mo stares at Rose then looks all around the room. I hide behind Rose's neck. It must tickle because she drops the mop.

"Gosh, you are clumsy," Aunt Mo says, her voice softer. She picks up the mop. "I'll finish here. Why don't you go in my studio and do some painting? It might help you settle in."

Rose groans quietly.

I flick her. I want to paint!

"Okay," Rose says, rubbing her neck. "Thanks."

"Great!" Aunt Mo says, looking confused at the sudden change of heart.

We leave Aunt Mo with the sink flood and walk into another room. It's magical. Sunlight streams in through the big windows. There are pictures on all the walls and colourful pots cover every surface. They must be the paint. I think about squeezing the juice from my one sad holly berry. "Isn't this incredible?"

"I guess..." Rose says, "but first I need to know why were you washing yourself in the toilet?"

"Why would I not wash myself in it?" I ask.

"Do you know what a toilet is?"

Not wanting to look stupid I say, "Do you think I don't?"

Rose blushes. "Star, toilets are where humans go for pees and poos."

"What?! Why?" I cry. "That's disgusting!" First, they put their poo in bottles and now in a chair pool in their house?! Why don't they go in a hole outside? Rotten radishes! I've just washed myself in pee pee water! I try not to retch while Rose fills a container attached to the wall with water.

"This is a sink," she says, "and this is clean water. Why don't you have a wash and I'll get us some paper to paint on."

Rose leaves and I tentatively step into the water. It's warm and there are little bubbles floating on top that smell like the lavender from the garden. I sit down and the purple petals of my dress fan out.

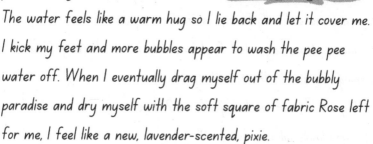

The water feels like a warm hug so I lie back and let it cover me. I kick my feet and more bubbles appear to wash the pee pee water off. When I eventually drag myself out of the bubbly paradise and dry myself with the soft square of fabric Rose left for me, I feel like a new, lavender-scented, pixie.

"Over here," Rose calls. She's kneeling on the floor surrounded by paper and paint pots. I sit next to her and watch as she picks up a wooden stick with a bushy end. That'll be much better for painting with than my twig. Except Rose doesn't paint with it. She sucks the wooden end. Taps her forehead with it. Rolls it around on the floor. Puts it nowhere near the paper. I think I'm going to explode!

"Are you going to paint with that?" I ask in a high voice.

She hands me the brush. "Why don't you start?"

I hover, holding it like Rose held the mop.

I know exactly what I want to paint - daytime. I dip the brush into a pot labelled forest green and sweep it onto the paper for the grass, then add swirls of strawberry red for Aunt Mo's roses. I wonder how many strawberries are squished inside that pot. Splatters and blobs of cobalt blue, lemon yellow, crimson red, burnt orange and indigo become other flowers. Colour fills the paper. I stab the paintbrush into the pots one after the other. Rose quickly gives up trying to make me wash the brush in between. She finds another brush and paints the oak tree trunk. Together we dab on the leaves using five different greens. I ditch my brush and smear the paint on with my fingers. Rose watches while I use my hands and elbows to add spots and splodges of green. I'm quickly covered in paint, including my hair when an over-enthusiastic splodge leaves me face down in the picture.

Rose giggles and starts to add her own finger spots.

"I've got an idea," I say and lie down on a fresh piece of paper. When I jump up, I've left a painty pixie print.

"Oo, pretty," Rose cries and does a print of her hand next to it.

"Good one!" I shout.

We do it again and again on fresh paper. When I accidentally roll onto the floor, I leave a perfect pixie print. Excitedly, I do another one. And another.

"Star," Rose says, "I'm not sure we should paint on the floor. I'm already in trouble over the cake and the toilet."

"But it's so much fun!" I cry. "Doesn't Aunt Mo want you to paint? This is painting!"

I thrust my hands into strawberry red and indigo and shoot into the air. Arms out wide, I spin, faster and faster, spraying droplets of paint in a colourful indoor shower.

"Stop!" Rose says, in a voice I haven't heard her use. She sits down on the floor and I flutter over, hovering next to her.

"I didn't want to come here," she says, "but it was nice of Aunt Mo to let me visit. I don't want to upset her. And all this mess definitely will."

I look around at the paint-splattered room. I've got it wrong. Again. What if Rose doesn't like me now? "I'm sorry," I say. "I got carried away."

Rose uses wet rags to clean the worst of the paint from the floor (and walls and ceiling). I drag our paper paintings to one side of the room and have my second lavender bath of the day.

"Much better," she says, looking happier.

"Rose?" I ask.

"Mm hmm."

"I really am sorry."

"You're forgiven," she says, smiling.

"This is the best adventure I've ever had," I say.

"Me too."

"Do you want to have more of an adventure?" I ask her.

"Somewhere we won't get into any trouble."

"What do you mean?" Rose asks.

"Let's go further," I say. "Past the garden. Past Aunt Mo's house. I want to see what's out there!"

Beyond Aunt Mo's

"This house is on a busy street," Rose says. "Are you sure that's a good idea?"

"I'm sure," I say, feeling brave. "This might be my only chance."

Rose hugs herself. "We'd need to sneak out."

"I have to see what's there." I really do.

Rose nods. She disappears and comes back with something to hide me in - her gathering bag, or rucksack as she calls it.

"Aunt Mo's still in the bathroom," she says, gesturing for me to climb into the rucksack. "We should go now."

Is this what having a friend is like? Someone that forgives you when you make a mistake? Someone to have adventures with? Someone who'll pretend they flooded the pee pee chair, so their aunt doesn't find out about night pixies?

The rucksack smells like apples. Before I climb in, I look up at Rose. "Thank you, friend."

She smiles so much that dimples appear in her cheeks. She leaves the zip open at the top so I can peek out, and we make our way down a corridor to another door. I'm about to see the whole world. Rose slowly pushes the handle down and edges the door open. She steps outside but instead of feeling excited I'm instantly overwhelmed.

Rose is right. It is busy. And big. And noisy.

I have to duck back into the rucksack for a minute before I'm brave enough to take another look. There are lots and lots of houses. All with doors painted different colours and windows looking straight at me. And there are people everywhere, talking and walking and stopping and starting.

A hundred different smells fight to get my attention: animals, smoke, food and so many new human ones. It makes my head spin, but not as much as the huge colourful things that keep thundering past.

My ears wiggle and I whimper.

"They're cars," Rose whispers. "There's a park at the top of the street, we'll go there."

The park is quieter and green. I feel brave again and embarrassed about being scared.

Rose sits on a wooden bench and places the rucksack next to her. "You're safe to come out," she says, "but be careful."

My wings bristle. She's only saying that because I was scared. For a second. "You don't have to tell me to be careful," I say, clambering out. I've had enough of being told what to do, or not do.

"I'm just looking out for you," Rose says. "I'm going to go and get an ice cream." She leaves abruptly, taking her rucksack. I watch her walk over to a big white car with colourful pictures stuck all over it and a window in the side. I've upset my first friend. I'll say sorry when she comes back. Rose is amazing and she's right, I do need to be careful.

I did it though: I've gone beyond the garden, beyond Aunt Mo's

47

house, in the daytime! I sit back on the bench and enjoy the sun on my face. If I can do this, I'm sure we can manage to move Granny. Maybe Rose could help us. We could go somewhere it's safe to go out in the night and the day. Mum might even give it a try. Life could be about to change.

"Kxxsss!"

My daydream is interrupted by a spitting cat. Murphy! "Go away!" I tell him.

"Kxxsss!" He hops up onto the bench and his claws come out. "Kxxsss!"

"Fine," I say. "I'll go." I soar up, away from the bench.

In the garden, Mum doesn't like me to fly above fence height. Here, I go higher than I've ever gone before. I look down at the park and over at Aunt Mo's garden with our oak tree standing proudly. It looks out of place with so many houses around it. I wonder what life was like when there were -

CRASH! Something bangs into me. I feel a sharp pain in my side, then wind rushing in my face.

9

Day Is Danger

It takes me a second to realise what's happened. A bird's got me. I'm braced against it and moving fast, but I manage to wrench my head round and take a look. It's black and doesn't look like any bird I've ever seen, or had Mum warn me about. It's smooth and shiny with two legs but no feet, one huge eye, and four spinning wings. And it's making a horrible buzzing noise.

I don't think this is a bird.

I'm stuck on its eye. If I can just edge downwards, I'll slip off. It takes every drop of pixie determination to move, no further than a daisy petal at a time, until I manage to slide off the not-a-bird.

I spin as I fall through the air. I can't figure out which way is up, and I'm so frightened that my wings refuse to work. Is this it? Am I going to end up a blob on the ground? With Mum and Granny not knowing where I am and Rose annoyed at me?

No, I am not! I flap and struggle and concentrate, and about a pixie's height before I hit the ground, I manage to hover, then land on my feet. I did it!

I'm back in the park!

A deafening buzz interrupts my celebration.

SMACK!

I'm knocked over and the black, buzzing not-a-bird pins me down in the grass.

"What are you?" a scratchy voice asks. A sticky hand picks me up and brings me to their face. It's a boy with squinting eyes. "Are you a fairy?!" he asks. His breath smells like dead animal. "A-mazing!"

"Give her back!" Rose shouts, running over, dropping her ice cream on the way. "Leave her alone!"

The boy pushes Rose and she falls heavily to the ground. "She's my fairy, I found her!" he shouts.

I try and bite him, but I can't move my head low enough. I can't move anything.

Rose tries again, grabbing at me, but the boy whips me away from her, squeezing tighter, so I can't help but let out a sob.

"I'm getting help!" I hear Rose shout.

"No! Don't leave me here!" I rasp and watch her run away. The boy's grip is so tight it's hard to breathe.

Mum was right. Day is danger. Humans do want to trap us. I'm so frightened I imagine I can see Mum and Granny coming to rescue me. Granny toddles along with her stick, ignoring Mum who keeps pointing back towards home. Our lovely safe oak tree. Why didn't I listen?

I imagine Mum flying towards me. She looks so real.

"Put her down!" she screams at the boy.

She sounds so real too.

"More! There's more of you!" the boy yells. "Wait until I tell everyone about this!"

She is real! Mum's here!

She bops the boy on the nose. He looks surprised but doesn't loosen his grip. So she sticks her foot in his ear, and that makes him loosen me just enough to get an arm out. But it also makes him angry. He swats at Mum and sends her flying. Think, Star, think!

"Excuse me," I say loudly.

He pulls me up to his face. "What?" he asks.

"This!" I shout, and stuff my free fist up his nose.

It's hairy and slimy but worth it because he loosens his grip in surprise, and I get my other arm free. He starts to go pink, then red, before his head jerks back and, "AH-CHOO!" Snot shoots out of his nose and, SPLAT! hits me, straight in the face.

I cough and splutter and the boy's disgusting bogies drip down my neck. It's super gross but also super slippy! I wriggle and squirm and eventually manage to wrench myself free, hitting the ground with a bump before I manage to get my wings working.

"FLY!" screams Granny's voice next to me and without thinking I grab her arm and start pulling her down the hill, towards Aunt Mo's house. I glance back and see Mum flying away from the boy. He stuffs something in his back pocket and starts to chase us.

"Leave me!" Granny puffs.

"Never!" I cry.

"Never," Mum repeats, joining us.

Together we half-drag, half-carry Granny down the hill as fast as we can. I can see Rose and Aunt Mo running towards us and feel the pounding footsteps of the boy behind.

Rose and Aunt Mo reach us first. Rose drops her rucksack next to me and hisses, "Get in."

I move towards it and Mum grabs my arm. "What are you doing?!"

"She's my friend," I cry, trying to pull Mum into the rucksack.

"Your what?!"

Have you got another plan?" I wail, pointing behind us.

Mum turns to look at the boy closing in, and immediately helps Granny clamber into the rucksack. I dive in after them and try not to scream as Rose pulls the zip shut and flings the rucksack onto her back. We tumble around in the dark before finally coming to a stop.

I'm sitting on top of Mum. She pulls me into a hug. "I was so worried, Star," she cries, her face in my hair. "I woke up and you weren't there. I thought you were gone forever, like Dad. We've been searching for hours!"

She pulls a daisy leaf out from her gathering bag and starts wiping the boy's snot off me. For once I let her fuss. Then she holds me away from her. "What were you thinking? Day is danger! Why don't you listen? And what's this about a human friend?"

I'm almost relieved when a second later a horrible smell distracts everyone.

"Sorry," Granny says. "I had dandelion tea last night."

Suddenly, we hear the boy's voice above us. "Give me back my fairies!"

It isn't Rose who speaks next, it's Aunt Mo. "Hello, Ralph. How are you?"

"I want my fairies," Ralph says. "Finders, keepers. Give them back."

"Fairies?" Aunt Mo says. "Aren't you a little old to believe in those?"

"I know what I saw, and I know she's got them in that bag," Ralph snaps, "and so do you."

Mum and Granny each grab hold of one of my hands and we all stare up towards the voices.

"I think you're mistaken." We hear Aunt Mo say. "I don't think anyone would believe that."

"They probably wouldn't," Ralph says, "if I didn't have drone footage of one of them. It's going to make me rich."

"Who's Drone?" Mum whispers. "And what have his feet got to

do with anything?"

"Footage?" Rose asks, her voice faltering. She sounds scared.

"Yeah," Ralph says. "One of them got caught on my drone when I was filming. Its face was right up in the camera. I'm going to show the whole world."

10
Moving Pictures

Tumbled together in the bottom of the rucksack, Mum, Granny and I stare through the darkness at each other.

Video. Footage. The not-a-bird has moving pictures of me and this boy is going to show everyone! Mum worked so hard to protect our family from daytime, and I've ruined it in one morning. Without saying anything I shoot up to the top of the rucksack and wrestle the zips apart so I can squeeze out.

"Star, no!" Mum cries, but I have to go. I have to fix this.

I clamber out onto Rose's back. She and Aunt Mo are still talking to Ralph, trying to persuade him to give them the footage. I wonder when Rose had time to tell Aunt Mo about the night pixies living in her garden.

The not-a-bird is sitting on the bench. I fly over. Somehow, I have to make the moving pictures inside it disappear. Rose is the one that knows about them, not me. Maybe I could make the whole not-a-bird disappear instead?

I can't see anything on it to make it move though, and it's so heavy, pushing with all my strength does nothing.

"Please can you fly away and never come back?" I ask it in desperation. Nothing. Nipping nettles! This is hopeless.

I hear a familiar, "Kxxsss!" It's Murphy, pestering a squirrel until it escapes up a tree. He saunters over to Ralph and rubs himself against his leg. Of course Murphy likes Ralph. A flash of black sticking out the back of Ralph's trousers catches my eye. I remember him shoving something in his pocket when he chased after us. It's the same shiny black as the not-a-bird. Could it be the answer?

I flutter over silently. Ralph doesn't notice me. He's too busy raving about how much money news networks will give him for a world exclusive on his fairy discovery. Murphy, however, does notice me.

"Kxxsss! Kxxsss!" he hisses, leaping up at me, his claws sinking into Ralph's leg.

"Owww!" Ralph shrieks, jumping backwards.

Murphy scales Ralph to get to me while Ralph dances around, trying to shake him off, and Rose dives in to rescue the crazed cat.

The kerfuffle lets me haul the shiny black box out of his pocket. It's so heavy it pulls me straight down to the ground.

I channel all my fear, strength and determination into dragging it back to the bench.

The box has a stick with a little ball on top of it and three circles to press. I jump on each circle and the not-a-bird makes a whirring sound.

It's working!

I stand on one of the circles and lean against the stick. The not-a-bird rises off the bench, straight up into the sky.

I'm doing it!

Except now that I've managed to make it move, I realise the not-a-bird flying away isn't enough. What if someone finds it? I need to know the moving pictures are gone forever. The only person who can do that is Rose and she's busy with Ralph. At least the screeching has stopped so I can think.

"Hey, pixie-trapper!" I shout as loud as I can.

Ralph turns around and sees me with his box. He storms over, Murphy following. I'm going to have to move fast. I jump to another circle, pull the stick towards me, and wish on every star in the beautiful night sky that this works.

Behind Ralph, the not-a-bird crashes back down to earth and drags along the grass towards Rose and Aunt Mo!

But will Rose know what to do?

I leave the box and soar upwards just as Ralph reaches me.

"What are you doing?" he cries, grabbing at me.

I hover just out of his reach.

Behind him I can see Rose fiddling with the not-a-bird.

Ralph snatches the black box off the ground and turns around just as Rose gives me a thumbs up.

Aunt Mo

Before Ralph can react, I dart over and land on Rose's shoulder. She drops the not-a-bird.

"Come along now, Rose," Aunt Mo says, and I jump down into the rucksack.

It's zipped up before Granny cries, "Ooft!" as I land on her head.

"Sorry," I whisper, pulling her and Mum into a hug.

Above us Aunt Mo says, "Walk fast. Don't look back."

We roll around inside the rucksack, but I can still make out Ralph's voice shouting in the distance. "Where's my footage? What did you do?!"

The next time we see light is when the rucksack is unzipped and Rose's face peers in. "It's okay," she says. "We're back home. You're safe."

I get up stiffly and move towards her.

"Star, no!" Mum cries, grabbing holding of my hand. The bravery she found to save me from Ralph has disappeared. She's back to

63

fearing daytime.

"We can't live in this rucksack," I say. "It'll be fine. Rose is my friend. She won't let anything bad happen."

"She's a human," Mum cries.

"She is," I say. "A human that saved us all."

"It's not just her out there, though, is it?" Mum replies.

"It will be fine. I promise." I pull my hand free and clamber out onto the kitchen table. The guilt cake is still there. It's been tidied up around the edges but still has a pixie shaped dent in the middle. For a second, I'm tempted to jump back in, but I don't think that would help the situation.

Aunt Mo is there too, looking at me. Her face is flushed. She keeps tucking and untucking her hair behind her ears, like she doesn't know what to do with herself.

Mum and Granny crawl out of the rucksack behind me. Granny struggles to get up. Once she's managed to straighten herself out, we all hold hands, me in the middle. I can feel Mum shaking.

I look at Aunt Mo and take a deep breath. "I just wanted to say, thank you, for helping Rose get us out of there. And sorry about the cake, and the toilet, and your paints."

Aunt Mo looks at Rose, who shrugs, and I realise she must have

taken the blame for the paint mess too. "It's okay," Aunt Mo says. "To be honest, I'm relieved it wasn't Rose. I was starting to worry. I want her to feel happy here."

Rose gives Aunt Mo a shy hug, and Aunt Mo gives her a huge one in return.

Next to me Mum hisses, "What are cakes and toilets and what did you do to them?"

"I'll tell you later," I whisper. I hope there is a later. Aunt Mo is coming closer. Granny squeezes my hand tightly.

"You're welcome to as much cake as you want," Aunt Mo says. "I don't really understand what happened in the bathroom, but I'm sure you didn't mean to do it, and the studio, well...." Aunt Mo pauses and tucks her hair behind her ears again. "You certainly made your mark, but I love the paintings. Did you both do them?"

"Yes," Rose says and Aunt Mo beams.

"That painting there?" Granny asks. "The one of us?"

She's pointing to the picture on the kitchen wall. The one that's dark blue with a swirl in the middle and three yellow dots.

"No.... not that one...." I murmur, looking more closely at it. Now that Granny has said it, I can't unsee our oak tree.

I look straight at Aunt Mo. Rose is staring at her too, her mouth hanging open.

"Did you know about us? Before today?" I ask.

Aunt Mo nods.

Everyone looks at Aunt Mo, then Rose looks at me, then Granny and Mum look at each other, and no-one says anything until eventually Aunt Mo says, "How about we all have some chocolate cake? It's a bit squished, but it still tastes good. My brother does make good cake."

Mum nods and Aunt Mo cuts two big slices and three small pieces of squished guilt cake. Rose and Aunt Mo sit on chairs, Mum and I sit on the table, and Granny sits on a biscuit tin.

"So," Mum says shakily, "you knew we were living in the oak tree?"

"Yes," Aunt Mo replies.

"For how long?" Mum asks.

"Well, I've always lived here," Aunt Mo says. "This house was the first to be built. I first saw one of you....you, I think," she looks at Granny, "when I was maybe five."

"And you didn't tell anyone?" Rose asks.

"Oh, I told everyone," Aunt Mo says, "but no-one believed me. Then, as I got older, I wondered if perhaps you'd rather people didn't know. You seemed keen to keep yourselves to yourselves -"

"What is this heaven?!" Granny interrupts. She's just taken her first bite of cake. "Brambles and bilberries! This is incredible!"

"It's chocolate cake," I say knowledgeably.

"It's....it's....it's....there aren't words," Mum says, cramming some into her mouth.

"So, you've been watching my family all this time?" I ask Aunt Mo. I don't think Mum and Granny are listening anymore. Granny has just put her whole face into the cake.

"Yes," Aunt Mo says. "At first because I was curious, then because I was worried about you. So many houses were built around us, I wasn't sure how you'd cope. And then I thought there was one less of you."

Mum's head snaps up.

Aunt Mo carries on. "I promised myself I'd do what I could to look after you. I never go in the garden at night, keep my lights off, grow lots of edible plants."

Mum relaxes. If Aunt Mo is going to all this trouble to look after us there's no way she's the one that took Dad. I wonder if I could get Rose to request no more radishes.

"And now?" I ask.

Aunt Mo gives me a warm smile. "I won't tell a soul. Ever. If you'd like to visit Rose and I, that would be, well, wonderful, but even if you'd rather not, my lips are sealed."

"My lips are so happy," Granny hoots from her pile of crumbs.

Aunt Mo laughs. "When you're ready to go I'll put some in a bag for you, but stay as long as you like."

"We'll stay until Star has finished cleaning up her mess," Mum says, giving me one of her looks. "And when we get back to the tree, we've some talking to do."

12
Night and Day Pixie

I know Rose is here because the curtains in her room are closed tonight. I stay up after the sun creeps out and Mum and Granny are ready for bed.

"Be careful," Mum says.

"I will," I say and don't even get a little bit annoyed.

After a looooong talk, Mum agreed to give me lessons on keeping safe and has slowly been letting me out more. It helps knowing Aunt Mo has been keeping an eye out for me. I went out for the longest time yet yesterday. I didn't tell Mum, but I escaped from a squirrel.

"Have fun," Granny says and gives me a wink.

I head up the tunnel and into the treehouse. Rose is there, waiting for me.

"Star!" she cries. "I'm so happy to see you!"

"You too," I reply, smiling. "I've been checking your window every night."

Rose laughs. "Mum and Dad don't understand why I suddenly want to come to Aunt Mo's so much. Get comfy, I've things to show you."

She opens her rucksack. A whiff of apple floats over before another wonderfully familiar smell hits my nostrils. "Chocolate cake!" I squeal.

Rose takes out a box with a ginormous slice. She tips it onto a plate and cuts me a piece, making sure I get plenty of icing. "Tuck in, but that isn't the best thing I've brought."

Nothing is as good as chocolate cake.

She pulls out a huge purple square.

I try and look impressed. "What is it?"

"It's a cushion!" she says. "You sit on it and it's super comfy. I borrowed it from home; we've got loads. Try it!"

I put my cake down reluctantly and climb onto the purple mound. "Oh wow! It's like sitting on sixty layers of moss!"

"This is going to be the best treehouse ever by the time we're finished," Rose says, smiling as I clamber back down to my cake.

"Are you ready for more news?" she asks, her voice high.

I nod, my mouth full of chocolate icing.

She squeaks and pulls out a letter. Then shakes it out and makes sure I'm looking before she reads, "Congratulations on coming first in the Woodside Primary School Art Competition." She stares at me, wide-eyed. "We won, Star!"

Not for the first time, I haven't got a clue what Rose is talking about.

"Remember Aunt Mo said our paintings were good. Well, I entered the one we did of the garden, and it came first!!"

"That's great, Rose," I say. I still don't really understand, but I'm glad she's happy.

"Star, someone thought our painting was so good they're going to give us a present!"

I cough and chocolate crumbs spray onto the treehouse floor. "A present for our painting?"

"Yes!" Rose cries. "And you won't believe what it is - a humongous paint set!"

"With proper paints? And brushes?" I ask.

"So many paints and brushes. We'll be able to paint the whole inside of the treehouse! And I've been thinking - it would make a

73

great background for my videos. We could make moving pictures together. But I'll never show anyone, not like Ralph!"

I drop my cake and fly into a spin. Paints and brushes just for us! Me and Rose painting the treehouse!

"There's something else," Rose says.

I'm not sure anything can make me happier than I am right now.

"The prize giving is at my school. I was wondering if you wanted to come? We could have another adventure."

I stop spinning. I don't know what school is, but another adventure sounds amazing. I was wrong, something has made me even happier. "You bet your buttercups I want to come!"

Acknowledgements

The Night Pixie is my debut children's book, and there are some people I owe a huge thank you to for helping me get here:

Sarah Hewlett and Katy Beighton from HB Publishing House for saying yes. You haven't just made the dream I've been chasing for a long time a reality, you've made it an absolute joy.

Chris White for bringing the story to life with your glorious illustrations.

My awesome SCBWI Misfits critique group for the feedback over the years. I've learnt so much from you all. Special mentions to longtime coordinator, Linda MacMillan, and chief cheerleader, Sarah Broadley.

The Scottish Book Trust for picking me as a New Writers Awardee and championing me ever since. You made me believe I could do it. Special shout outs to my brilliant mentor, Juliette Forrest, and all round legend, Lynsey Rogers.

WriteMentor for helping me find my young fiction posse, aka The Mildreds. Your critiques and encouragement have been invaluable.

Heather, Karis, Jenna and Emily Hutchison and Jenny van Hooff for reading/being read the book and sharing your thoughts.
Lou Treleaven for your helpful feedback and encouragement.

My mum and dad for your support and igniting my love of books with those early library trips.

My best friend and sanity maintainer, Anna Boag.

And by far the biggest thank you goes to my incredible husband, Jeff, and wonderful children, Ruaridh and Immy, for supporting my dream without question, and always saying yes when asked, 'Could you have a wee read of this poem/chapter/entire book?' I love you more.

Hazel Knox

The Night Pixie Series continues...

Join Star in the next book as she visits Rose's school, makes an unexpected friend and dives into another chaotic adventure.

Let's be friends...

www.hbpublishinghouse.co.uk

 hb_publishing_house

 HB Publishing House

 hb_publishing_house